Space
Pirates

David Orme

Illustrated by
Paul Savage

Contents

Badger Publishing

Chapter 1 - A Big Problem

"Engineering! Report, please! Todd, what's going on?"

It had been quiet on the bridge of the Nightstar. The cargo ship almost flew itself on long journeys between the stars. There wasn't much for the captain and crew to do. Until now.

The ship gave a sudden shudder. Then the red warning lights started to flash. Captain Street quickly checked the control panel, but nothing showed up. The spaceship flew on.

Todd reported back from the engine room.

"I don't understand it. The warp engine cut out, then started again. It's never done that before."

"What do you think we should do?" asked the Captain.

"I'd like to shut down the engine and check it out. It shouldn't take long."

"OK. Report back when it's done."

The crew on the bridge listened for the deep hum of the warp engine to die away, but nothing changed. At last, Todd spoke again.

"Captain, we've got a problem. I can't shut down the computer. It's locked me out. It's running a program. It's as if something has taken it over!"

Just then Tess broke in. She was in charge of the ship's radio.

"There's a powerful radio signal coming in. It's sending computer code!"

There was only one explanation.

Someone was taking over the ship!
Something had to be done, quickly.

"Todd, knock out the fuses on the main power supply," ordered Captain Street.

This was a dangerous thing to do. The crew's life support needed the power. But they had to get control of the ship.

"Knocking out fuses now."

There was a terrible yell from the engine room.

"Todd, what's happened? Are you OK?"

It took a long time for Todd to reply.

"I'm OK, captain. But only just. I got a huge shock from the power supply. Whatever it is doesn't want me to shut down the computer."

"Captain, look at this!"

Baz, the ship's navigator, was staring at a computer screen in alarm.

"There's another ship out there. That must be where the radio signal is coming from. And that's not all. It's making us change course, and there's nothing I can do about it."

"What's the new course?"

Baz checked, and checked again.

"It's bad news. We're heading straight for the Ghost Nebula!"

Chapter 2 - Into the Nebula

Space was full of dangers, but nebulas were the greatest danger of all. Nebulas were huge clouds of gas and stars. The dust and gas was spread very thinly, but because spaceships travelled so fast they could cause great damage. Worse, the gases were charged with electricity. This stopped the ships' computers working.

"How long till we reach the edge of the nebula?" asked Captain Street.

"About two hours," replied Baz.

The Ghost Nebula stretched across the view screen. White arms of glowing gas reached out towards them like a poisonous spider. Inside the nebula, misty looking stars shone with many colours.

"Look there," Baz said suddenly. "There's a way into the nebula that's clear of gas. That's where they are taking us."

An hour later they entered the dark pathway through the nebula. On and on they went, following the mysterious spaceship that had captured them. At last they saw a bright star.

"That star has planets," said Baz. "That must be where we're going."

Then two things happened. The first was that the ship started to slow down.

The second was the sound of air being pumped out into space.

"Someone's trying to kill us!" said Captain Street. "Space suits on, then down to the cargo bay, quickly!"

"What's the plan?"

"Don't argue, just do it!"

The Nightstar crew were lucky. The cargo was equipment to set up a new space station in orbit round a planet. One piece of cargo was a landing craft, used to travel up to the space station from the planet's surface. It had its own life support system.

By the time they got to the cargo bay there was no air left in the ship.

Their suits would only give them air for a couple of hours. Without the lander, they could not survive.

Todd opened the giant cargo airlock. Outside, the great nebula was glowing.

"Inside the lander, quick!"

Captain Street took the controls. Carefully, she guided the lander out of the airlock door.

"Where are we heading, Captain?" asked Todd.

"We don't have the fuel to make for open space. We've no choice. It's that planet, or death!"

Chapter 3 - Space Pirates

Baz checked the surface of the planet through the long distance viewer.

"Look at that!"

They all looked at the screen. The planet was like Earth, with blue seas and deep green forests. But Baz had worked out the direction the Nightstar was taking and had seen something else.

"Near that mountain range. It's a space port. There must be a dozen spaceships there. What's going on?"

Captain Street looked grimly at the screen.

"Space pirates! Ships have been going missing lately - too many. No one would ever think of looking for pirates in a nebula. That radio control gadget is clever, too. There's a brain behind this, and I think I can guess who it belongs to."

"So can I," said Todd. "It must be Drake!"

Doctor Drake had been a great scientist once. But he had become a criminal. Four years ago he had been sent to the space prison on Mars. Two years ago he had escaped. No one had seen him since.

They watched as the Nightstar was carefully guided down onto the space port.

"They'll get a big surprise when they find there's no crew!" grinned Todd.

"They'll see the open cargo door. They may think we were sucked out into space. We'll wait until night, then land in the forest about five miles from the base.

"We'll walk from there. It's important they don't know we're on the planet."

"Have you got a plan, Captain?"

"No but I'm open to ideas!"

***

It was a long, hard walk. The alien forest was dark and threatening. In the distance, they could hear the sound of huge beasts roaring, and the screams of their victims.

The space suits were difficult to walk in, but at least they made sure that insects couldn't bite them. They could breathe the planet's air, but their helmets had special filters to remove any dangerous viruses.

At last they saw bright lights ahead of them. They had reached the edge of the space port.

Chapter 4 - The Sleepy Guard

The pirates had put up bright lights around the field. Spaceships they had captured stood dark and empty. Near to one side was the pirates' own ship. The air lock was open.

"The Nightstar is over there. Look! They're fetching out the cargo now."

Four men were heading into the air lock. At that moment, Captain Street knew what they had to do.

"Head for the pirate ship!"

They ran around the side of the space port, trying to avoid the lights in case they were seen. In a few minutes they had reached the air lock of the pirate ship.

"Todd, stay out here and keep watch. We'll go in and see what's going on."

They crept up to the bridge. A man was sitting back in a chair, feet up on the control desk. He seemed to be having a snooze. It wasn't Drake. Captain Street guessed the scientist himself must be on the Nightstar. This man must have been left to guard the control desk. He wasn't doing a very good job.

Baz crept forward and grabbed the pirate round the neck. He almost fell out of his chair with shock. The pirate reached down for a weapon, but Captain Street got there first, kicking it away from him.

In one corner there was a pile of stores.

Tess found a coil of thick wire.

"This will do to tie him up."

But the pirate didn't want to be tied up. He kicked and yelled, even when Captain Street threatened him with his own gun. They all held him down, and managed to tie him up at last.

They were so busy doing this that they didn't notice a door slowly opening on the other side of the bridge.

"That's enough. Stand away from that man. Now."

A tall, grey haired man stood in the doorway. It was Doctor Drake.

Chapter 5 - Dr Drake in Control

The scientist was
carrying a strange
weapon. There was
nothing they could do.
They moved away
from the man they
had tied up. He
seemed more scared
of Dr Drake than they
were. He knew he had
let him down.

Dr Drake spoke into a radio. "Have you
cleared the ship yet? Stay where you
are for the moment. We've got visitors.
I'm going to send them for a little ride."

He suddenly noticed that Baz was
looking carefully at the control panel.

"You! Come away from there! Outside, all of you!"

"What about me?" asked the other pirate. He was still tied up. "Aren't you going to untie me?"

"No. You can stay like that as a punishment for being useless!"

He turned to the Nightstar crew. "Now, move, and don't try anything!"

Captain Street, Baz and Tess did what they were told. The weapon Dr Drake held looked deadly.

He marched them out of the spaceship and across the space port to the Nightstar.

"I'm going to send you on an interesting journey. No-one has ever gone into the centre of a nebula. That's where you're going!"

Captain Street was angry with herself. She was in charge, but she had let her crew down.

"Why don't you just kill us now and be done with it?"

"Much too messy, Captain. Now, get on board."

But there was a problem. When they reached the Nightstar, the air lock door was locked shut.

It was Dr Drake's turn to be angry. He spoke into his radio.

"What is going on? Open the air lock, you fools!"

Slowly, the air lock door swung open. And there stood Todd, with a pirate's gun in each hand.

Chapter 6 - Doctor Takes a Ride

"You didn't expect me, did you, Doctor? Don't worry, Captain. I haven't joined the pirates!"

Dr Drake stepped back in astonishment. Tess took her chance. With a high kick she knocked the weapon out of the scientist's hand.

Todd had heard Baz, Tess and the captain coming out of the pirate ship. He had managed to slip across to the Nightstar before they got there.

"You need to feed your men better, Dr Drake. I found them having a meal from our ship's supplies. They had put their weapons down first, ready for me to find!"

"Where are they now?" asked Captain Street.

"I've locked them in the storeroom. They don't seem to like it in there!"

They could hear banging and shouting coming from the storeroom.

"Well done, Todd! I think Dr Drake had better join them. He might be able to shut them up!"

Captain Street turned to the scientist. "I think it's your turn to take a ride, Doctor, but I think you'll find it's a lot more boring than the one you promised me!"

**

Baz soon found out how the pirate's radio control system worked. A few hours later the pirate ship took off - with Captain Street at the controls.

The Nightstar, with the pirates still on board, took off too - carefully controlled by Baz from the bridge of the pirate ship. It followed them out of the nebula, and on a course back to Earth.

Captain Street spoke to the pirates on the ship's radio.

"It's going to take a week to get back to Earth, so I hope you've managed to get out of the storeroom by now. If not, you're going to get a bit hungry. But don't worry. I'm sure there'll be a good meal waiting for you when you arrive at the space prison!"